One Moose, Twenty Mice

Clare Beaton

BAREFOOT BOOKS
BATH

one moose,
but where's the cat?

two crabs,
but where's the cat?

three ladybirds,
but where's the cat?

four whales,
but where's the cat?

five horses,
but where's the cat?

six ducks,
but where's the cat?

seven snakes,
but where's the cat?

eight frogs, but where's the cat?

nine parrots, but where's the cat?

10

ten tigers,

but where's the cat?

**eleven owls,
but where's the cat?**

twelve fish,
but where's the cat?

thirteen monkeys,
but where's
the cat?

fourteen dogs, but where's the cat?

15 fifteen dolphins,

but where's the cat?

sixteen spiders,
but where's
the cat?

seventeen hens, but where's the cat?

eighteen butterflies,
but where's the cat?

nineteen elephants, but where's the cat?

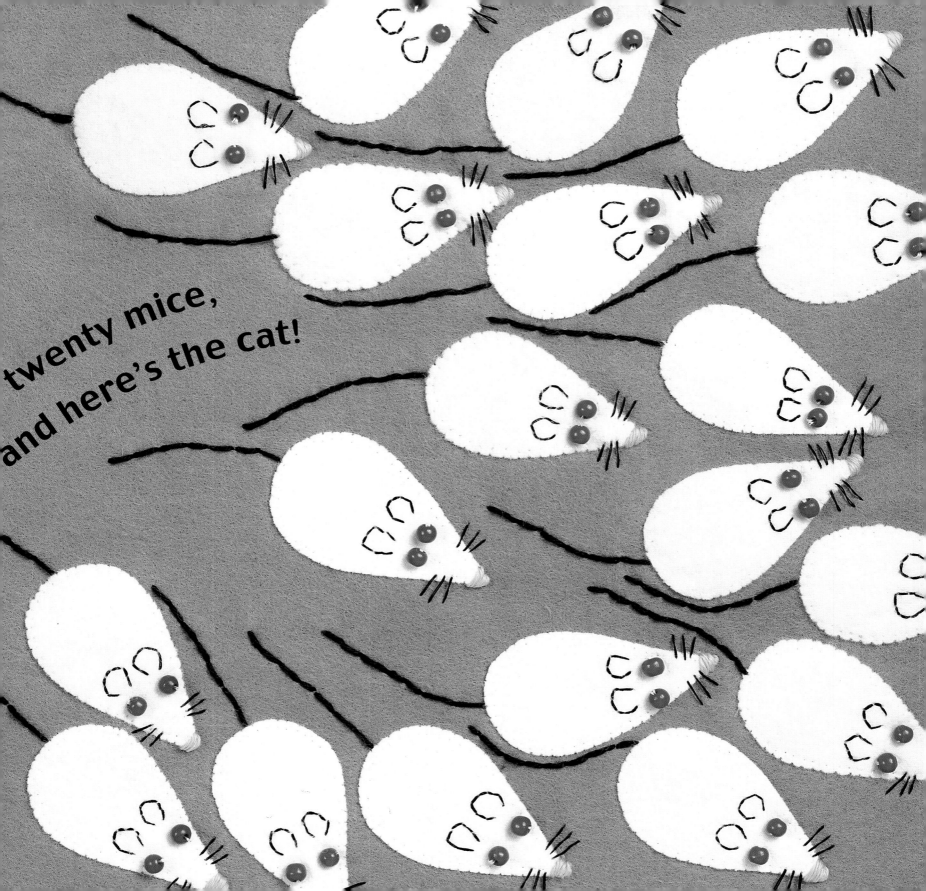

twenty mice,
and here's the cat!

Barefoot Beginners
an imprint of
Barefoot Books
PO Box 95
Kingswood
Bristol BS30 5BH

Hardback ISBN 1 902283 10 4
Paperback ISBN 1 902283 38 4

Graphic design by AG Design
Colour reproduction by Grafiscan, Verona
Printed in Singapore by Tien Wah Press (Pte) Ltd.

1 3 5 7 9 8 6 4 2

BAREFOOT BOOKS publishes high-quality picture books for children of all ages and specialises in the work of artists and writers from many cultures. If you have enjoyed this book and would like to receive a copy of our current catalogue, please contact our London office —

tel: 0171 704 6492 fax: 0171 359 5798

e-mail: sales@barefoot-books.com website: www.barefoot-books.com